Brenton

Shifter Ink, Volume 1

S L Davies

Published by S L Davies, 2022.

BRENTON

First edition. September 15, 2022.

ISBN: 979-8215421840

Written by S L Davies.

Hendrix

It was cold. So, fucking cold. Probably didn't help that I didn't have many clothes left. It felt like every day more of my clothes were stripped from me. Whenever I got back to my sleepout more of my shit had been taken. If I found out who was taking my stuff, I'd fuck them up. I snorted at the thought. I couldn't fuck up an ant in the state I was in.

My skin was itching, the scabs on my face were bleeding. My teeth were rotting and ached in my gums every time that wind swept through me. The heroin ate at my body more than my healing could keep up. I knew that if I could get clean for a little while, my teeth and the scores of open wounds on my body would heal. *But that was the problem, wasn't it?* I had to get clean for that to happen.

I bent forward and wrapped my arms around my body as I marched against the howling wind that whipped through the Melbourne streets. I was on a mission to find my dealer. He'd been getting harder to find recently and I wondered who he owed money to, this time. This was the problem with having a dealer whose brains were scrambled from using his own gear. But he always had the best stuff.

I'd checked all his usual haunts, which meant that I was going to have to search in the more unsavory places. The places I hated going. The back alleys were often filled with any number of supernaturals ready to roll you for whatever you had in your pocket. It was where the more desperate of us hung out. Those that were too fucked up to even be able to break into houses and steal shit to sell, chose to stay. Instead, they would wait for unsuspecting victims exploring the city to wander down the alley and then rob them with blood-filled syringes.

It was a fucked-up head space to be in. Heroin was a cruel mistress; she took and took. She gave, but her high was fleeting and all too quickly we would have to be back to searching down another hit. Over and over the cycle would continue. Every junkie wanted to be clean, none of us didn't look at ourselves and liked what we saw. It's part of the reason we stayed high so that we didn't have to think about who we had become. But this world, being homeless, surrounded by the underbelly of a faceless city, wasn't built to keep us clean. The pull back to our queen was always strong. Too strong to avoid.

I kept my head down as my mind raced, I felt myself becoming erratic the more need for the pinch of the needle and burn of the drug I had. Every step hurt. My skin itched like there were thousands of unseen bugs crawling all over me. Even my hair hurt. My eyes roved every dark corner as I walked alley after alley. I ignored the cries of the hookers who faked their orgasms for dealers and pimps. I ignored the slap of skin as thugs punched into unsuspecting tourists who happened on their activities. I ignored it all as I searched.

Desperation was beginning to bite at me as I finally rounded the corner to see, Rick huddled in a corner. His eyes were wide and roved all over the alley. He looked terrified. I walked towards him. Rick looked up at me and his eyes widened; he shook his head wildly. Rick pushed himself deeper into the corner. Rolling my eyes I continued towards him, whatever he was on, had him paranoid.

"You can't be here," he hissed.

"Come on Rick, I need gear," I groaned.

Rick shook his head. "Jesus, Hendrix, don't you get it, you can't be here. I'm telling you for your own fucking good."

"What are you fucking talking about? Have you got gear or not?"

Rick growled and shook his head. "Get the fuck out of here Hendrix, fucking find another dealer."

"What the fuck?" I spat. I was about to get in Rick's face and demand to know what the fuck was going on when I heard the one voice that could send fear down the strongest of men.

"Ah Richard McLane, I've been looking for you," Cillian Purcell said with a chuckle. I gasped and stepped away from Rick quickly.

Cillian Purcell ran the streets. There wasn't a man that could send fear into another quite like him. The dragon shifter was big, scary, and as cruel as they could come. Cillian spared me a look but didn't say anything. I took off down the alleyway but was stopped by two of his goons.

"Where you going junkie?" one of them sneered.

"Please, I'll go," I said with a tremble in my voice.

The one that spoke chuckled. "No, no, stay, party with us."

They held firm onto my arms. I didn't have the strength to fight them. Not only were they much bigger than me, but I was coming down hard. I had no strength left in me to fight. The one that had hold of me turned me around and I could see Cillian standing over Rick.

Rick was pleading, but Cillian stood sneering down at the weasel shifter like he was nothing more than a piece of shit under his shoe.

"Here is the problem, Richard. I don't like people who get in my business. I don't like people who get into business with me and then don't give me the money they owe me. And Richard you fit into that category, don't you?"

Rick shook his head; his eyes were wide with fear, and I could see sweat starting to bead on the side of his head. My stomach curled as I tried to think of a way to get out of this situation. But there was no way out. My head was racing and yet I couldn't grasp hold of a single thought.

"Please Cillian," Rick pleaded.

"Please Cillian," Cillian imitated. "You are fucking pathetic."

Faster than even my eyes could catch up; Cillian reached out to Rick and literally tore his head from his body. My stomach revolted and I bent forward vomiting at my feet.

"Fucking hell," my captor groaned. "You chucked on my fucking shoes."

I groaned, but it was enough for the two thugs to have let me go. I took the chance; I didn't even think about it. I took off as fast as I could. Calling my broonie as best I could through the haze of my panic and withdrawals, I felt my body shrink as I ran. I didn't stop. I heard Cillian roar at his thugs to get me, but I didn't stop. Taking advantage of my size I ran through a small crack in the wall of the nearest building. Breathing heavily, I watched as the men ran past the hole in the wall. I wrapped my arms around my chest and shook with fear.

I was fucked. I was a dead man. I had to get out of Melbourne. I had to find somewhere new, and I had to start all over again. My brain was screaming at me to run. I had no idea where to. I had literally enough money to get maybe a bus and maybe a meal or a deal whichever I found first if I was lucky. I was in withdrawals, and I knew it was only going to get worse. Tears prickled at my eyes and started to work down my cheeks. I was fucked. *Why was this my fucking life?*

Chapter One

Brenton

The sound of the tattoo gun buzzed. I loved it as background noise. It was something I think I would never tire of. I had found my family when I joined Shifter Ink. Burgess was an amazing employer and every single person that worked there was one of my best friends. I'd been so lost for so many years. I'd wandered all over the world, looking for my place, it hadn't been easy.

I was now almost eighty-five years old. Of course, to humans that is ancient. I should be rocking in a nursing home and using a walker to get about. But to vampires, I was still a young man. I was seventy-eight when I finally found Shifter Ink. I hadn't even heard of Lalbert until early in my seventy-eighth year. I'd lived all over the world, experienced so much, but something deep inside me always wanted to find my home.

I'd been desperate to find that place I belonged. My family was scattered everywhere. My Mother and Father were somewhere in the city of London. I hadn't spoken to them since I first left home at sixteen. My father a drug-addicted, abusive piece of shit, I was glad to get out of there. My mother was also a junkie, but she wasn't cruel. Just neglectful. I had brothers and sisters but wouldn't even know if they were still alive or where they would be. We'd all scattered, left our parents to their drugs.

On my travels, I always looked out for those on the streets. I had put more drug addicts into rehabilitation than I could count. I didn't do it for the thanks or the hero status. I did it because I wanted to see a better world. This place was so fucking cruel and if I could make a small difference in someone's world then I was prepared for it.

When I came to Lalbert, I was surprised to see that there weren't too many rough sleepers. That didn't mean that the town was completely devoid of trouble. There were still problems with drugs.

There was still crime. It happened, I think even in a town of two people, one would be a criminal. It happened. World over.

During the day I would spend it tattooing and with my Shifter Ink family, then of a night, I would go out with bags of food. I had the places that I visited. Along the river always drew many of the rough sleepers. I made sure they had tents, warm sleeping bags, and enough food to get through. Some of them were drug-addicted, some were homeless through unfortunate circumstances and others chose that lifestyle. I never judged their story, I just wanted to help them to live a little easier.

I'd made some great friends as a result. They called me the protector of Lalbert. It was a title that made me embarrassed at first, but now I owned it. I liked to think that I kept those that needed protection safe. And I never asked for anything in return. It took a while for some of them to trust me, but once they realized I wasn't there to take anything from them, and they wouldn't owe me for their protection they quickly began to trust me.

Some of them would even seek me out if they or someone they knew were in trouble. That was when I knew that I'd made an impact. When they would come to the shop with a worry about one of their friends and family. A lot of people might look down on the homeless but really, they were a family just trying to make the best out of their lives.

"Alright, love, you are all done," I said as I wiped the excess ink off the skin of the fae that sat in the seat in front of me. A little blonde girl getting her first tattoo. She'd sat well, considering she'd chosen her ribs to be tattooed on. I'd tried to talk her out of that position, but she was adamant. "Hop up slowly so that your head doesn't spin and then go over to the mirror and have a look."

Shael slowly stood from the bed and walked over to the mirror. She gasped and her eyes widened. I'd never get sick of seeing that look on my client's faces when they first took in their tattoos. I lived for it.

"Brenton," she gasped. "I fucking love it."

I chuckled. "I'm glad. Come on back over and I'll wrap you up."

Shael practically bounced back towards me. I pulled out the roll of the second skin and wrapped it over the tattoo after smothering the art in healing cream. With her fae healing, it wouldn't take long for her body to accept the tattoo and it to heal.

"Leave this on for the night then you will be able to take the second skin off and just use the cream when it's needed. The tattoo will be healed in about two days," I said.

"Thank you so much. You're the best. I'm going to tell all my friends that they must come and see you," she said.

"Oi, what about me?" Orion, one of the other artists pouted making Shael laugh.

"I'm sure they will want to try out all of you," she replied.

Orion grinned and went back to the client that he was working on. "Alright love, let's get you fixed up and then you can go and show everyone your art."

And that was how it went. Every day I got the opportunity to do what I loved. I got to create beautiful art for people. Each piece meant something different to everyone. I loved hearing the stories and meeting each client. My life was complete. Fulfilled.

Chapter Two

Hendrix

"Hey mate, wake up," the bus driver pulled me out of my sleep. I looked up at him with bleary eyes. I didn't have a clue where I was, I'd waited in the hole in the wall for hours until I felt I was safe. Quickly I'd dashed back to where my clothes were dropped, checking that my money was still in my pocket. I got dressed and ran for the bus station. I'd kept an eye over my shoulder the whole way. I'd bought a ticket for the soonest leaving bus and got on. It wasn't until the bus was on the outskirts of Melbourne that I finally began to relax.

"Where am I?" I asked. My head was fuzzy. I was itching everywhere, and all my joints ached. I desperately wanted a hit. But I didn't even know the first place to look for more gear. It wasn't like dealers just roamed the streets with neon signs pointing them out.

The bus driver frowned. "Lalbert. Listen, are you in some sort of trouble?"

I gasped and shook my head. "No, no, I'm fine. Sorry for being late to get off," I mumbled as I stood quickly and felt my head spin with dizziness.

"Woah," the bus driver said as he reached out a hand to steady me. "Look, head down to the river, if you follow this road straight down, you'll find the river. The rough sleepers all are down there, there might be a dealer down there that you can get some stuff to help you feel better. Otherwise, the hospital is across the road."

I sighed and nodded my head. "You reckon there will be a dealer down at the river?"

The bus driver sighed and frowned. "I don't know. They've been doing a lot to clean it all up, so maybe. But possibly not."

My shoulders deflated. I was just going to have to wait it out. I knew that the withdrawals and pain were going to get worse before it got better, but what other choice did I have.

"Thanks," I murmured as I pushed past the bus driver and stepped off into the street. Lalbert. I'd never even heard of the place. It was a small town. Not so small that it would be easy for Cillian to find me if he came looking. But not big enough to get lost in either. I bit into my lip as I glanced over at the hospital and thought about heading over there. Maybe I could fake an injury or something and they would give me enough to tide me over.

I scrubbed my hands at my face and shook my head. They'd never believe it. I was dirty, I couldn't even remember the last time I'd showered. I looked down the road to where the bus driver told me that the river was located. At least if I headed down there it would give me a chance to wash and maybe I'd find some food on the way.

I wrapped my arms around my middle and started down the road. The fear of Cillian still weighed heavily on my mind and every sound had me jumping. I continually looked over my shoulder expecting his thugs to jump out and grab me. I tried to stay in the shadows as best as possible.

The town was surrounded by leafy forests. Behind me, there was what appeared to be the main area. Large buildings and bright lights shone from the various shops and businesses. It didn't take long before I reached the river. In amongst the trees, I could see tents scattered. The odd flash of light of someone lighting up flickered through the trees. I spotted the odd campfire and could hear voices.

"Hey, you new here?" A voice said, startling me and causing me to yelp. "Sorry, didn't mean to scare you."

I looked at the man that seemed to materialize out of the tree line. I shook my head and blinked my eyes.

"You mute?" he asked with amusement.

I shook my head again. "No. Yeah, I just got here. Do you know where I can get gear?"

The man shook his head. "Fresh outta luck here mate. The last dealer got chased off by the protector."

I frowned and sighed. "Thanks."

"What's your name?" the man asked.

"Why do you wanna know?" I questioned back.

The man chuckled and shook his head. "I don't really, but you look like you need a friend."

"I need a hit," I replied.

The man chuckled again and nodded his head before reaching into his pocket. "Here, don't fucking tell a soul."

I looked down at his hand which held a small baggie filled with white powder. "What is it?" I asked.

"Meth," he replied.

"What do you want for it?" I asked.

The man shook his head. "Nothing man. Just take care of yourself and if you meet the protector, take him up on his help."

I frowned and looked down at the man's hand again. I weighed up if this was a trick or not. I wasn't sure what to do.

"I'll just leave it here. Do with it what you want," the man said as he placed the baggie down on the ground and walked away, seeming to materialize back into the tree line and disappear. I blinked hard, wondering if I'd just imagined what happened.

Walking over to where the man had left the baggie I bent down and picked it up. It was real. I opened the bag and sniffed at it. There was no mistaking that smell. I reached into my back pocket where I kept my kit. It was just a small plastic bag filled with a spoon, lighter, and needle. I went into the trees and sat down on the ground with my back against a tree. Pulling out the spoon I carefully as I could with trembling hands poured the contents of the baggie onto the spoon. My body was racing with excitement. Flicking the lighter on I waited impatiently for the meth to turn to liquid under the head of the lighter.

Once it was liquid, I pulled my needle out and filled the syringe with the liquid, letting it cool slightly before finding a vein that hadn't collapsed. No sooner did the drugs hit my system than the euphoria took over. I leaned back against the tree trunk and closed my eyes. Sweet relief washed over me. I was going to be alright. With the drugs in my system, I was indestructible. Cillian wouldn't be able to touch me.

Chapter Three

Brenton

I looked down into the eyes of the girl at my feet as she licked up the underside of my cock. Groaning, my eyes rolled, and my head tilted as she swallowed the head of my cock, swirling her tongue as her mouth moved up and down my shaft.

Her fingers scratched lightly over my balls and taint. I thrust my hands into her hair and moved her mouth up and down, delighting in the beautiful sounds she made as my cock pushed deep into her throat. Her eyes watered with every gag.

I moved my hips back and looked down at her red lips that were coated in saliva, which dripped down her chin. I reached out and took her hand, silently leading her over to my couch. We'd only just made it in the front door before we were both naked and getting busy.

I didn't even know her name. She was just a random pick-up from the bar. We both wanted one thing and we both knew what it meant. We'd get each other off, she would go home, and I'd have empty balls.

I sat on the couch and guided her to straddle my lap. She looked down at me with a small smile on her face. Her eyes blazed red as she sunk down onto my cock. Her pussy grasped hold of me, and I gasped at the tightness.

"Fuck," I grunted as she rocked forward, resting her hands on my shoulders she moved me in and out of her. I clasped my hands on her ass and squeezed the skin tight. The girl moaned and dipped her head into my neck. I felt her fangs run over my neck in warning.

"Bite," I instructed with a heady growl.

I'd no sooner let the word fall from my lips than I felt her fangs sink into my neck. My cock swelled and my orgasm took over my body. I roared as sprays of cum splashed inside her. The girl let go of my neck and tipped her head back. A drip of blood dribbled down her chin as she cried out in orgasm. I leaned forward, taking her nipple in my mouth, and letting my fangs pierce the skin, drawing her orgasm longer.

Lifting my mouth off the wound, I licked at the sweet blood and watched as the bite mark healed. She looked down at me with a bright smile before pressing a quick kiss on my lips. The girl climbed off my lap and went to her clothes that we'd dropped at the front door.

"Thanks, that was fun," she said as she got dressed and I heard the door open.

"It sure was, love," I said with a smile as I glanced over at the door in time for her to exit and close the door behind her.

I smiled and leaned back in my chair, kicking my feet up on the coffee table in front of me, I scrubbed my hand down over my chest. I hadn't intended to pick up at the bar, I'd only gone there for a quick meal and a drink. But she had come out of nowhere. She was after one thing, the same thing that I was willing to give. The only thing I was willing to give. A quick fuck, nothing else.

I wasn't in the market for a relationship. It wasn't that I wasn't interested, it was just that I'd never met anyone that really pulled at me. I never had to search hard for a bed partner, or really a couch partner. I never fucked in my bed, it got too messy. The men and women that made it to my bed always wanted to stay. They seemed to get this idea that because they were in my bed, meant I changed my mind on what we had going on.

I closed my eyes and stretched, letting out a yawn. It had been a long day; I'd had a lot of clients. I loved what I did, but every now and then we got one of those clients that just sucked all our energy.

A knock on the door roused me. I stood and went to where my jeans had been tossed. Sliding them on my body, I swung the door open. Zach Smith stood on the other side. He was one of the first guys I'd met when I came to Lalbert.

"Hey, Zach, what's up?" I asked as I stepped out of the way so that he could come in.

"I'm not here to stay, but I just wanted to let you know, we've got a new one in town."

Zach was a bus driver who drove between Melbourne and Lalbert. He would often come and let me know when someone who was a rough sleeper came into town. It allowed me to go and find them, introduce myself and see if they needed anything.

I nodded my head. "Down at the river?"

"Yeah, he is pretty fucked up though. He was withdrawing bad. He was looking for gear, but he headed towards the river," Zach replied.

I winced. We didn't often get badly drug-addicted people coming to Lalbert. They tended to stay in the big cities. For this guy to come to Lalbert without a supply of gear told me he was running from something.

"Thanks, mate. I'll go and find him. Give you a name?"

Zach shook his head. "Na. You won't miss him. Broonie, tiny little thing, wild and filled with fear."

"Omega?"

"Na, alpha."

I nodded my head and reached over to my shirt, slipping it on. I knew that I wasn't going to be able to sleep until I did something to find the guy.

"How old do you reckon?" I asked.

"No older than twenty, maybe. But hard to tell for sure."

"Alright, I'll go and see if I can find him. Do you know if Ryan is still working down at the river?"

Ryan was a local drug dealer. I didn't like him, but I also recognized that if we got rid of all the drug dealers, the addicts would move on to find new ones, potentially running themselves into trouble. So, I turned my eyes from him and didn't chase him off. He was the only one that I let stay, and that was only because I knew the gear he sold was at least good stuff, it wasn't filled with shit that would kill the addicts.

"Yeah, last I heard," Zach replied.

I reached out to my boots and slipped them onto my feet. "If the bloke ended up down there, then Ryan is likely to have seen him. He pretty much knows everything that goes on down there."

"Yeah, I hope you find him, he was pretty fucked up," Zach said with a sigh.

I winced. Nobody started taking drugs because they had a good life. Every drug addict I'd ever met came from a shit life. They'd had to fight just to live. I wondered what this guy's story was.

"Alright, thanks man, I'll go search for him. Thank you for letting me know."

Zach nodded and gave me a smile before following me out the door and heading away with a wave. I sighed and looked down the street. I'd purposely chosen a house that wasn't far from the river, it gave me a chance to keep an eye on everything. It also allowed those that were needing help to find me easily. Now I had to go in search of some kid that may or may not have gone to the river. Like looking for a needle in a haystack.

Chapter Four

Hendrix

I felt like I was invincible. That meth was the best I'd ever been given. It kicked ass over the shit that Rick had. That was why I never bothered using his meth, I always relied on the heroin, but this stuff had me feeling like a superhero.

I walked down to the river. I could see tents and a campfire in the distance but decided to stay away from the people. I felt like I was invincible, that didn't mean I was. Stripping out of my clothes I waded into the center of the river, feeling the rocks stab at my feet. The water was freezing, and my skin prickled as the cold penetrated my body. Once I was deep enough that the water was about waist high, I ducked my upper body.

Breathing heavily, I pushed myself to stay under the water with just my head showing. My mind was moving so fast, I had so much energy. I ducked my head under the water and opened my eyes. I couldn't see anything in the darkness. Lifting my feet from the bottom I pushed along the surface of the water, remembering those brief swimming lessons I had once when I was a kid.

Kicking my feet, I let the current push me along. Under the water, there was no fear. My lungs started to burn with the need to get air, but I pushed it further. I wondered how long it would take before my body just took over and made me breathe. Lifting my face from the water I splashed my arms and legs like a dog would and sucked in a deep breath before pulling my head back under the water.

The current pushed me along the river and for the first time in so long, I finally felt free. There was no pain, no fear, nothing. Just me and the water. I rolled onto my back and kept my eyes closed, allowing the water to wash me downstream. I had no idea where I would end up, but at that moment I didn't care. I didn't give my clothes a thought, I was free.

Suddenly I felt my body come to a screaming halt as pain burst through my skull. My eyes flung open, and my vision instantly blurred. Darkness crept into the edges of my mind, and I tried to think what had happened. But through the drug haze, I couldn't work it out. The meth though did its job, it took the pain away instantly and I smiled once more, closing my eyes. This time though the darkness was deeper. It sucked me under, and I found myself floating, no longer on the water but in darkness so dark that it was terrifying.

I tried to scream, but it felt like my mouth was filled with water. Nothing came out but a gurgle. I tried to open my eyes, but they wouldn't open. Suddenly hands grabbed at my body, I spun myself around searching for the source of the hands, but I couldn't see anything.

I screamed again but the sound was so far away that it didn't sound like it was coming from me. Slowly the darkness pulled me deeper. There was no peace though. Some darkness brings peace, but not this one. Instead, I found myself in what appeared to be a cave, on a huge screen on one wall of the cave played a movie.

The closer I looked at the screen, the more I realized that the movie that was playing was my life. I saw myself as a chubby baby. I didn't know how I knew that baby was me. I had no memory of myself as a baby. I didn't remember my parents. All I remembered was being on the street, discarded like a piece of trash.

But in the movie, there was a father and mother. They both looked down at the baby with such tenderness and love. The mother gently wiped her fingers down the baby's cheeks, making him smile and gurgle up at her. I smiled as I got lost in the scene. I wondered who those people were. I wondered if they were my parents and where they had gone.

Suddenly the scene changed, and I watched as a five-year-old me got shoved onto the street after the first foster father I remember had beaten me. He'd whipped me so hard that my body was broken and bleeding. All because I was hungry and dared to steal a piece of bread.

I stared at the screen with tears in my eyes. Curling my legs to my chest I held onto myself. My life only got worse. I watched as that little boy ran through the streets, searching for something, someone to love him and protect him. Instead, he found men and women prepared to take from him. I watched as the little boy ate from the garbage bins that dotted the public streets and hid in the bushes of public parks.

No one took any notice. No-one stopped to ask where his parents were, instead that little boy became another face in a sea of faces. The scene changed again, this time the boy was grown, he was a teenager, and he was standing beside his first dealer.

Jamie. A warthog shifter. The one that taught him how to break into houses. I rocked back and forth on my side as I watched myself as a teenager break into the first house. I had been so frightened. Jamie told me not to come back without some valuables or he would kill me. I believed he would too. He said I owed him, the drugs he gave me to make things not hurt anymore. I owed him, to make me forget.

The darkness enveloped me again, this time sucking me under until there was nothing but silence surrounding me. And this might have been the most terrifying place of all.

Chapter Five

B renton
    I walked down to the river and past the row of trees where I knew that most of the rough sleepers spent their time. Keeping my eyes open, I looked through the woods in hope of finding the new arrival.

"Protector," Ryan called from behind me.

I stopped and turned to face him. "Ryan, I heard we have a newcomer, he was looking for drugs, have you found him?"

Ryan nodded his head. "Yeah, about an hour ago."

"Did he get the gear off you?"

Ryan nodded again. "Meth, I gave him only enough to get him through tonight, and then I hoped that I'd be able to see you in the morning."

"Alright, did you see where he went?"

Ryan shook his head but glanced over to the western side of the river where it turned a bit wilder. I nodded my head and thanked Ryan with a wave before I headed towards the western side of the river. As I trekked along the path, I saw that there were clothes strewn across a rock on the very edge of the river.

Going over to the clothes, I picked up the pair of ratty jeans and a t-shirt that was filled with holes and looked like it hadn't been washed in months. I was careful as I plucked through the pockets of the jeans. There was a pouch filled with drug paraphernalia and a wallet in the other pocket.

Opening the wallet, I noticed that there were about twenty dollars in cash and a single ID card. Pulling out the card, I glanced down at the name, Hendrix Witter. There was an address listed in Melbourne for him. I didn't know the address, but that wasn't surprising. Hendrix though had to be the guy I was looking for.

I scanned the surface of the water but couldn't see him in the river. I glanced up and down the edge of the river. But there was no sign of him. Worry started to form in my gut as I thought about a drugged-up kid possibly drowning. Chewing on my lip I let out a shaky sigh. This didn't look like it was going to end well.

Walking along the path in the direction that the river flowed I kept watching the surface of the water. If he had drowned, his body would eventually resurface, I didn't know how long that would take to happen though. I passed through the bracken that covered the edge of the river and cursed as the thorns pricked my legs, but I couldn't stop. I knew that the rapids were coming along just around the corner.

On the surface, the river appeared to be calm, but the current moved quite quickly. Once someone hit the rapids though, it could completely knock them off balance. The rocks that were under the water were sharp and could easily do damage.

I rounded the corner just in time to see Hendrix floating on his back waving his hands in the air. I went to call out his name just as his entire body crumpled. He splashed in the water briefly before his body went still and began to sink.

"Fuck," I roared as I raced down to the river's edge and didn't give it another thought. Wading into the water the icy cold took my breath away. I couldn't see Hendrix on the surface of the water and knew that he could be anywhere.

The saving grace of being a vampire at that moment was my ability to see in the dark. I sucked in a deep breath just as I reached the rapids and ducked under the water. The spray coming off the rocks buffeted me around and I had to dig my feet into the loose soil to stay upright.

I opened my eyes under the water and searched frantically for any sign of Hendrix. I was about to run out of air when I spotted the pale leg that floated lifelessly between the rocks and a fallen branch. Lifting my face out of the water and sucking in a deep breath of air I pushed through the current to where Hendrix was.

His body was twisted, and I could see that he had scrapes and cuts on his upper torso. When I was finally able to reach him, I clasped onto his cold arm. He was so thin that the bones crunched together under the firm hold I had on his arm. I tugged him towards me and winced as a large gash formed in his leg. Thankfully, he was supernatural, and the wounds would heal faster.

Hendrix was completely unconscious and when I was able to pull his body close to mine, I could see why. A large gash crested across the top of his head and was dripping a steady stream of blood. I had to get him out of the water and his wounds patched up enough that they would stop bleeding.

Wading back through the current, pushing with all my strength I finally made it to the edge of the river and was able to pull Hendrix out. Once we were on firm ground, I lifted the boy into my arms and carried him back towards the camps. They didn't have much, but I knew that Hendrix needed heat, and something to bandage his head. I would be able to replace clothes later if necessary.

As soon as I reached the edge of the campsite one of the younger rough sleepers, Adam looked up and gasped.

"Shit, he doesn't look good, bring him over here," he said moving aside from the log. "Doc, we need you."

The older man who we knew as Doc came out of his tent grumbling, but as soon as he saw the state that Hendrix was in, he dashed over to where I sat, holding the boy to my chest.

"Alright, we first need to warm him up, he is at risk of hypothermia. Adam bring my sleeping bag and one of the wool blankets. Are the only major wounds he has on his head and leg?"

I nodded my head. "Yeah, from what I can tell."

"What the hell was he doing?" Adam said as he came over carrying Doc's sleeping bag and blanket.

"He is a drug addict, he had meth, and obviously thought it a clever idea to go for a swim," I reply.

"Shit," Adam said with a shake of his head. "What else do you need Doc?"

"Something to wrap his head and leg. We need to stop the bleeding until his healing can kick in," Doc replied.

Adam nodded his head and dashed back into his tent before coming out with a tourniquet and a t-shirt. "For his leg," Adam said holding up the tourniquet before looking over at me. "I haven't used it, it's from before, I kept it because I thought if I ever got bit by a snake."

I nodded and gave the kid a smile. "I trust you."

Adam smiled but then looked back at Hendrix with all seriousness. "He's been using a long while."

"Yeah, I think so. Hopefully, he survives this, and then we can do something to help him."

"I know you will be able to help, protector. You helped me and everyone that comes down here."

I smiled and nodded. But I was never sure.

Chapter Six

Hendrix

I blinked my eyes open. I was wrapped tight in blankets. Frowning I glanced around the room that I was in. I didn't remember how I got here. My brain was firing with danger signals. Alarm bells were going off. *Why couldn't I remember?* I took a deep breath and closed my eyes as I set my mind back.

Cillian, I remember Cillian coming for Rick. Ripping his head off. I remember running. The bus. But that was where everything went blurry. *Why couldn't I remember beyond that? Was I hurt? Was I in the hospital?* I opened my eyes again and glanced around. It wasn't a hospital room, well none that I ever knew of.

Lifting the blankets my frown deepened when I realized I was naked. *Had I sold my body?* It wouldn't be the first time to be able to afford drugs. My body didn't feel like it was coming down, it didn't feel that craving either. But then I didn't feel that same euphoria that I normally did when I had heroin in my system.

Suddenly a door swung open, and a vampire came into the room. He had red hair, a big red beard. He was tall, probably the tallest man I'd ever seen. I could tell he was an alpha and the way that he strode around the room told me that it was in his house that I lay.

I cleared my throat and drew the vampire's attention towards me. When he looked down at me, he smiled gently.

"Hey there. It's good to see you finally awake, I wasn't sure when your healing would help you," he said.

"Healing?" I questioned.

"You don't remember taking a swim in the river last night and nearly dying?"

My eyes widened and I shook my head. The vampire nodded his head and held up my jeans and t-shirt, before placing them on the bed.

"I've washed your clothes for you. Your wallet is there on the dresser. Do you know where you are?"

"Well, I know I'm probably in your house, but I don't know where that is," I replied.

The vampire nodded his head. "You are in a town called Lalbert. You came in on the bus from Melbourne yesterday. My name is Brenton. The bus driver came and told me about you and was worried about you. So, I went looking for you. You'd managed to find Ryan, our local dealer who gave you some meth. You decided to take a swim in the river but hit your head on the rocks in the rapids, knocked you out and then you nearly drowned. Doc and Adam were in the camp so were able to help me to save your life. I gave you some blood and brought you back here."

I reached up and touched my head, but my healing had taken care of the wound. There was nothing left. I blinked my eyes closed. I could've been killed. Cillian wouldn't have had to come for me after all, I would've done the job for him.

"What are you running from?" Brenton asked pulling me out of my thoughts.

My eyes snapped open, and I shook my head. "Nothing," I replied.

"Bullshit. Look, I look out for the supernaturals who find themselves homeless, I'm willing to help you. But you are running from something. People don't just happen across here from Melbourne, not without any gear on them and not knowing any of the local dealers. Zach told me that you asked him where a dealer was and Ryan said the same thing, so you didn't know anyone here."

I sighed and looked away from the intense stare of Brenton. "Why do you care anyway?"

"I care about everyone. I like to help people. You are young, so fucking young, too young to be so drug-addicted that you are prepared to inject anything that some dealer gives you."

I scoffed. "You don't even know me. I'm twenty, but you've no idea what has happened to me in those twenty years."

Brenton's stare was intense as he nodded his head. "You're right. I don't know what you've been through. But I've lived an exceptionally long time already. I came from drug-addicted parents, I've been on the streets since I was fifteen years old. I've lived all over the world; I've was homeless in many countries. Believe me when I say that I've seen just about everything you can imagine. Your story isn't unique, it isn't rare. Sadly, everything you could possibly tell me I've probably seen happen to at least twenty other kids or may have even had it happen to me."

I hummed in my throat. My story wasn't unique, I knew that. I had lost count of the number of others that I'd met whose story resembled mine. It was shit. The entire world was filled with shit. It didn't matter that there was more equality between supernaturals and humans, the world was still catered for humans. The governments were still run by humans and favored humans. It meant that when a supernatural kid was on the streets from five years old, most people turned their heads and didn't give a shit. It was just another problem that should be kicked under the rug and ignored.

I scratched at my face. "Why aren't I craving?" I asked.

"My blood. You will start to need more gear once my blood works through your system, but I'm here to make you an offer," Brenton said.

"What's that?" I asked narrowing my eyes. He wouldn't be the first piece of shit to try and offer me something.

"You can stay here as long as you want, I'll help you get clean and I will protect you from whatever you are running from, but you need to get clean, get a job, get a life," he said.

I snorted. "You can't protect me."

Brenton raised an eyebrow. "I beg to differ."

I nodded my head and closed my eyes before sighing. "And if I don't agree?"

"Then you walk out of here, you go find your own way on the streets and you spend the rest of your life running from whatever demons are chasing you."

I bit into my lip. I didn't know what to do. The thought of constantly being on the run from Cillian wasn't appealing.

"I'll leave you to think about it while I go and prepare some breakfast, then I must go to work. If you want to stay here then feel free to stay, if you are gone when I get home, I will know your decision."

Brenton went to the door. "Wait," I said causing him to stop and turn around. "You are going to just leave me here? What if I rob you?"

Brenton shrugged his shoulders. "If you do, then you do, but you will want to make sure you use whatever you steal to leave Lalbert because I will be tracking you down. But if you leave, you leave. It's up to you."

I frowned but nodded my head. Brenton nodded and turned to leave the room. I couldn't make sense of the guy. *Did he really mean it? Was he really going to let me stay? Was he really willing to trust me not to knock his shit off?* I didn't know what to do. I sighed and closed my eyes feeling a wave of exhaustion wash over me. Maybe I could just sleep for a little while.

Chapter Seven

B renton

Once Doc and I had managed to get Hendrix stable, I'd been able to give him some of my blood and then take him home. I washed and dried his clothes and gave Doc some extra blankets and a sleeping bag to replace the ones he'd used to warm up Hendrix. I also went and had a long shower to warm myself up from my impromptu dip in the icy river. Doc was a good man. I didn't know how it came to be that he found himself homeless. But he'd once been a doctor in the army, after seeing more war than reasonable, he came home a very different man.

Most of the homeless tended to avoid him. Except for Adam. Adam had latched onto Doc and not left him alone. I often wondered if they were fated mates, but they never said anything. Adam was only young, in his late teens, he said he didn't know his age completely. I didn't know his story either. It wasn't something I tended to ask, their story was personal and if they wanted to tell me they would.

I knew that Adam had grown up in a breeding facility but managed to escape when he was twelve. He'd been on the streets since. I had suggested to him to go and see the Devil's Advocates, they were an MC club that took in omegas that came from breeding facilities. Places that bred supernaturals to sell them to fights or just for nefarious reasons. Adam always said he was happier to be homeless. The kid was sweet, and I always watched out for him. I knew that he wasn't willing to leave Doc. Adam was the only guy that seemed to utterly understand Doc. But the pair of them were good people with shitty situations.

When I first met Adam, he was a lot like Hendrix, strung out on whatever drugs he could get his hands on. He was around seventeen when I first met him. I gave him the same ultimatum that I gave Hendrix that morning. He could stay, get clean and then do whatever he wanted with his life, but he had to stay clean, or he could just go on with his life. It took two months before Adam decided it was time for a change. Doc had found him overdosing on the edge of the river and brought him back to life. Doc pleaded with Adam to take me up on my help and he got clean.

It wasn't easy, shit, giving up any drug is never easy. He was in a lot of pain and wanted to give up more than once. But now he was a different kid. He still decided to stay homeless, living on the edge of the river, but I often wondered if that was for Doc's sake rather than his own. But Adam did have a job at the supermarket collecting shopping carts and returning them. It wasn't anything glamorous, but it paid alright money. Enough that it provided him and Doc with food and supplies that they needed. I checked on them every night to make sure they were safe.

Ryan knew not to sell to Adam, and he respected my rules on that. I know it's ironic to say that a drug dealer can be a good person, but Ryan was. I mean he still sells that shit, but he has a story and a reason too. I don't know Ryan's story, but I trust him to look out for the people that end up on the streets. It was a weird friendship we had, but it worked.

I'd checked in on Hendrix before I left for work but found that he was asleep again. I left him some breakfast that he could heat up easily in the microwave and plenty to drink and eat for the day. I suspected that he would spend most of the day sleeping on and off while he recovered from everything. He wouldn't start to crave more drugs until either later that night or in the morning so he had a little while before that would become the next problem.

I was curious to see if he was still going to be there when I got home. He wouldn't have been the first one that I'd reached out to T.and attempted to help that robbed me and taken off. It's why I didn't keep anything sentimental in the house. T. V's, computers all that kind of shit was easy to replace. Yeah, it still pissed me off, but it came with the territory, sometimes even scared dogs bite their owners.

That's what many of these kids were, they didn't understand that I wanted to help them. They often mistook my kindness as manipulation. It took them a while before it sunk in, but eventually, it did. With Adam, there was more than one time I woke to find him climbing into bed with me because he expected that I wanted to take from his body. After about the fifth time of me rejecting him, he finally understood that I didn't give because I expected something back from him in a physical sense. Seeing Adam clean and thriving was my reward, which was all I asked of him.

Once Adam got it, he became a different person. He opened to me a lot more. He was prepared to let me in past the walls that had previously been impenetrable. I didn't question him about his past, I never expected him to tell me his whole story, I wasn't a psychiatrist. That wasn't my job. My role in his life was a friend, someone that he could come to, no matter what the problem was. Someone who would protect him.

It's why I did what I did. For kids like Adam and men like Doc. To see them happy, despite living on the edge of the river, made me feel like I'd achieved. To see Adam clean meant the world to me. It gave me a purpose to wake up every morning. I recognized that not every kid like Adam was willing to be helped. For every success I had, I also had at least two failures. But I chose to focus on the wins. I just hoped that Hendrix would be one of those wins. I didn't know what it was about him, but he affected me. When I saw him unconscious and sinking in that freezing water my heart had just about leaped out of my chest.

He wouldn't have been the first kid I'd seen dead, but I couldn't explain what it was about Hendrix that made it so much more prudent for me to save him. I needed to get to him. Something was pushing me to save this kid. And as much as I didn't necessarily believe in fate, I still believed in that push that happened in my spirit. I just needed to save this kid. No matter what happened, I would always look out for him.

Chapter Eight

H endrix

When I woke up again and looked over at the time, I saw that it was just after one in the afternoon. My stomach was grumbling. I stretched in the bed. I couldn't remember the last time I slept in a bed. I considered staying hidden amongst the blankets, for the first time in an exceptionally long time I felt warm and safe. It was an unusual feeling. I listened to the sounds around me, but it was all silent.

Brenton said that he was going to work but I wondered if that was just a trick. My bladder reminded me that it was there, and I knew I wasn't going to be able to stay in bed for long. I glanced down and saw my jeans and t-shirt folded neatly on the bed. Slowly I moved my body and was in awe. I didn't hurt. *When was the last time I didn't hurt?* I didn't have any cravings, but it didn't feel like I had drugs in my system either. I could see why there were people out there that got addicted to vampire blood. If this was how it made me feel it could be my new addiction.

I placed my feet onto the carpeted floors and wriggled my toes. The comfort was strange but wonderful at the same time. I pulled my jeans over to me and slipped them on. They'd been washed. The last time they'd been washed would have been six months earlier when I had a spare pair of clothes and was able to find some coins to use a laundromat. I slipped the t-shirt over my head and stood from the bed. I tip-toed to the bedroom door and cracked it open just enough to look out into the hallway.

No movement sounded in the house. Part of me expected Brenton to jump out at any moment and beat me up or something horrible. But from what I could tell he really wasn't in the house. I slowly stepped out into the hallway and tip-toed to the next door. I swung it open and saw that it was another bedroom. This one appeared to be the main bedroom. The large bed was covered in dark bedding, the walls were dark and luxurious looking. I shut the door and continued to creep down the hallway. Another door showed me a linen closet before I finally opened the door to a bathroom.

It was bigger than any bathroom I remembered. There was a shower in one corner with a big deep bath along the other wall. A basin stood in the center of another wall with a toilet in the corner. I went to the bathroom and relieved myself before washing my hands and wiping my wet hands on my jeans. I glanced at the bath again. It was tempting to run a bath of warm water and soak in it, my stomach grumbled though, reminding me that it had been days since I last ate. I remembered Brenton saying that he was leaving me breakfast.

I exited the bathroom and crept back down the hallway, my whole body was on edge as I listened for any sounds that might tell me whether the vampire was still there. I made it into the living room which was a quaint room, filled with two couches and a chair. A large television sat against one wall. The blinds were pulled low, keeping the light in the room dim. Off the living room was a kitchen that was what I assumed was standard.

I went into the kitchen and opened the fridge. In a container with my name on it was what looked like bacon, eggs, sausage, and tomato. My stomach growled in hunger at the sight. I pulled the container out and read as best I could over the note Brenton had left on top. *Put in microwave for two minutes. Enjoy.* I read the note over and over. *Could he really be who he said he was? So fucking trusting?* I snorted and shook my head. Fucking stupid if he just takes junkies into his house and trusts them.

I placed the container in the microwave and followed his instructions, while I looked for a knife and fork in the drawers. By the time I found them the buzzer on the microwave sounded and when I opened the door, the scent of hot food washed over me. I couldn't even begin to remember the last time I had hot food, let alone fresh hot food. Normally I bin dived. This was a luxury to me.

I sat down at the bench seat and opened the lid of the container. I closed my eyes as the scent of cooked bacon and sausages washed over me. I didn't want to think that Brenton was for real, but if this is what he meant by allowing me to stay here to get clean, man I wouldn't even begin to know what to think about it.

The first bite of the food had me moaning. I gulped the food down until the container was empty, having never tasted anything so delicious in my life. Once I put the last morsel of bacon in my mouth I leaned back on the stool and rubbed over my belly, groaning with satisfaction.

I stood from the stool and took the container to the sink before searching for washing detergent and giving my dishes a wash and finding a glass to get myself a glass of water, before washing my cup. I thought briefly about taking off. I wondered if there was money still left behind in my wallet that Brenton had left on the dresser. I'd put it in my jeans without even checking. I reached into my back pocket and opened it to find that I still had my cash aside.

I noticed however that my kit was gone. That didn't surprise me. It wouldn't be the first one I lost. I glanced around at the house and wondered what to do. I bit into my bottom lip. If I stayed, I had to trust that Brenton was who he said he was. Or I could take off. *But to where?* I had only just got to Lalbert, I didn't remember the dealer who I got drugs off, I don't even remember where the river was that I apparently nearly died in. *Where could I go?* I couldn't go back to Melbourne, the whole reason I came here was to get away from Cillian. If I went back there, he would find me for sure.

I sighed. Exhaustion swept over me, and I considered going back to bed. Chewing on my thumb nail I continued to think over my options. I just didn't know what to do. Finally, after what felt like hours, I managed to come to the decision to go for a walk and see what Lalbert had to offer. My clothes were clean, at least I'd be able to sort of fit in, maybe. I searched the floor for my shoes and found them by the front door.

Slipping my joggers on my feet, I left through the front door, making sure to lock it behind me, and started to walk down the front path. The sun was high in the sky and warm on my skin. The houses were all nice neat suburban houses. To my left, I saw that it appeared to go to parklands and possibly the river, but to the right led to what looked like the city of Lalbert. Choosing to head towards the city, I took off at a brisk walk, this would give me time to think about what I could do, whether I moved on or came back here. Maybe if I came back, Brenton would have changed his mind and would tell me to move on. At least if that happened, I would have been able to scope out the town and know where I could hole up for the night.

Chapter Nine

B renton

I wasn't sure what to expect when I got home from work. I had thought there was a good possibility I would walk into my house to find that it had been completely cleaned out. However, when I walked in through the front door, I realized that the place was as I left it. I went into the kitchen and noticed that Hendrix had eaten and then cleaned up what I'd left for him for breakfast.

I kept walking down the hallway towards the spare bedroom. I gave the door a brief knock before opening it. The bed wasn't made, but Hendrix wasn't in the room. I walked back down to the living room and noticed that his shoes were gone from beside the front door.

I sighed and sat down on the couch. Well, I'd tried. I'd made the offer; I couldn't save everyone. It still hurt when they didn't take me up on my offer. I just hoped that Hendrix found peace. I stretched my arms high above my head and yawned. I'd had a late night and started early this morning, making sure that Hendrix was alright.

I still wanted to head down to the river to check on Adam and Doc. I needed to take Doc's sleeping back and blankets back to him that I'd brought home to wash. The people that I got to know all knew that they could come and bring their washing to my home any time. Adam and Doc usually came every week to do a load of washing and then I would drop it back into them once it was dry. It made me feel good knowing that at the very least their clothing and bedding were constantly clean.

I also organized haircuts for them, and they had the shower to use if they wanted it. Sometimes Adam came up for a bath, I wasn't sure what had happened to him, but I knew that he struggled with pain from time to time, especially in the cooler months, so he always relished a warm bath when he came up. I made sure to have fresh shampoo, conditioner, and bubble bath for them to use when they came here.

They might not want to live in a conventional house, but the least I could do was to make their life a little easier. It was a bit of selfishness on my part, helping made me feel good. Burgess's brother Asher would have a field day with that, he would say I had a servant kink. But it wasn't like that. I just liked helping where I couldn't help those that I loved.

I scrubbed my hands up over my face and groaned. Standing from the comfort of the couch, I went to where I'd packed Doc's sleeping bag and blankets into a bag. Grabbing the bag, I stepped out the front door into the dying sunlight, before heading towards the river. The last of the summer was here and it would all too soon turn cold. That's when I worried most about those that were rough sleepers.

I thought again of Hendrix. I wondered how long he'd been on the street. I wondered how many winters he'd had to endure in alleys or along rivers. I remembered the winters of London. It was awful. Australia never got that cold, which was a good thing, but if you weren't freezing you were soaked to the bone in London. Maybe that was why I never went back. I wasn't sure. But I made the decision that if I could stop someone living in the cold I would.

I was lost in thought by the time I reached the river. Memories floated through my mind, memories of doing what I could to survive. I didn't tell any of the people that I helped that I had an innate understanding of where they'd come from. I'd done everything to make money. It wasn't until I got hold of some sketch books and pencils that I realized I could draw. From there living became a little easier. I was able to sell my artwork, before getting some of it displayed in an art gallery. I was fortunate to meet my mentor, Barney Watson. He was an old artist, a phoenix shifter. He saw the work that I was peddling on the streets. He told me that I had immense talent and would like to show case my work.

At first, I was wary of the man, he was so eccentric. He wore a top hat and had a mustache that curled at the sides. His clothes were always made of expensive material. It took a while, but finally, I put my trust in Barney and he instantly took me under his wing. He gave me a room to board in his home, where I had access to an art studio, filled with so many materials I was in awe. He showed me techniques I never realized even existed.

I stayed with him for fifteen years, working under him, learning everything I could. Until one day I found him dead. He'd taken his own life. A note left beside his body told me that he was tired and had shown me everything he could, now it was time to make it on my own. I was destroyed. Police and ambulance members came through and tried to save his life, but it was no use. Barney was dead. I was lost and didn't know what to do. That same day, Barney's attorney came to me and said that Barney had left me everything, his entire fortune.

As it turned out, Barney wasn't just looking for a protégé, he was looking for an heir. He believed in fate. Something I struggled with. He believed that he was led into an area that I was in, an area that he never visited. It was fate that he found me. I was in a total state of shock as the attorney explained to me everything that Barney had left in my name. The attorney told me that Barney had given him his plan to take his life for me to live.

I was barely old enough to know what it was like to live on my own. I was thirty-five years old. It was a long time ago and Barney was a man that I would never forget. It was part of the reason I did what I did. To help those that needed help. I didn't live as eccentrically as Barney, I wasn't interested in flashing my wealth, but what I did want to do was to protect and care for those that were as lost as I was at twenty years old when Barney first found me on the streets.

Chapter Ten

Once I reached Doc and Adam's campsite, I noticed that they were sitting around the fire they'd just started. Ryan was sitting beside Doc while Doc regaled him with a story from when he was a child. I wasn't comfortable with Ryan coming around but so far, he'd been good at keeping his word and not selling to Adam.

"Protector," Doc said with a bright smile. "It's good to see you. How's our friend?"

I shrugged and sat down. "He was gone by the time I got home from work."

"You left him in your house alone?" Ryan asked with shock.

I looked over at him and smiled as I handed over the bag of bedding to Doc. "Yeah, I did."

Ryan snorted and shook his head. "Shit, man, you are more trusting than me. I can't tell whether you are amazing or just stupid."

I laughed. "Probably a little of both."

Ryan grinned and shook his head again. "Did he leave a note or anything?" Adam asked.

I shook my head. "No. Nothing. I gave him the choice to stay with me and get clean or he could leave, I'm not going to stop him."

Adam smiled sadly and shook his head. "I wish he'd taken you up on your offer. It helped me so much."

I shrugged my shoulders. "Not everyone will. I can't make them. I just hope that he is alright."

"On the run, you reckon?" Ryan asked.

I nodded my head and leaned back against the log I was sitting against. "Yeah. I don't know from what, he didn't say, but no one comes to Lalbert just to be homeless. And not withdrawing like Zach said he was."

Ryan nodded. "Yeah, he was in full withdrawal when I saw him. That's why I gave him the stuff, I knew that he was not doing well. I didn't expect him to go fucking swimming in the river though."

I waved my hand. "I know. Some people make some dumb choices. Shit, wouldn't have been the first dumb thing I'd done in my years."

Ryan chuckled and nodded. "Nor mine. Alright, guys, it was good chatting to you all, but I've gotta go. People to see and do as they say."

"Take care of yourself Ryan, and remember my offer still remains for you," I replied as Ryan stood from the log he was sitting on.

He stopped and looked down at me biting into his bottom lip before sighing and nodding his head. "Thanks, protector. See ya guys, and if I see the kid, I'll tell him that he is still welcome back to you."

"Thanks, man. That would be great," I replied with a smile.

I had got the feeling for a while that Ryan didn't want to sell drugs. He didn't like the life he was living but for whatever reason he was stuck. He never said anything about his past, he was as tight-lipped as the rest of us. But I still always gave him the option to hide him. I knew that the Devil's Advocates would help him disappear if he was in trouble. I would find a way to keep him safe. He just had to say the word.

"It's a real shame Hendrix left," Adam said with a sigh.

I nodded my head. "Yeah, I'm disappointed. But hopefully, he will get the help when he is ready and maybe he will come back."

"Maybe," Adam sighed as he leaned his head on Doc's arm and closed his eyes.

We sat in silence staring into the fire, soaking in its warmth and the last of the sun's rays. I could sometimes see the benefits of sleeping rough on days like today. The sun, the sound of the river, the birds singing their goodnight songs, and some friends. If only it was always this easy.

"Alright guys, I just wanted to bring back Doc's bedding," I said as I stood from the ground and dusted my pants off.

"Here, let me get you the sleeping bag and blankets you gave me last night," Doc said.

I waved my hand and shook my head. "Don't worry about it, Doc. Keep it as a spare. That one that you've got is thin. The cold will be coming soon."

"Thank you, Brenton. You're a good man," Doc said with a nod and smile.

"Thank you, Doc. Take care of each other and if you need anything, you both know where I live," I said before turning and leaving.

My mind was still firmly on Hendrix as I walked home. I rounded the fence of my property and walked up towards the front door before coming to a complete stand still. Hendrix was sitting on my front steps. His chin rested on his knees and his arms were wrapped around his legs. He looked so young and tiny sitting there.

"Hendrix? You alright?" I asked.

Hendrix looked up at me and gave me a small smile. "I was hoping that you were telling the truth about wanting to help me."

I smiled and nodded my head. "Come on in man, I'm telling the truth."

Hendrix stood and I unlocked my front door before waving him inside. Hendrix walked through the door with nervous energy pouring off him. This was a big step, and probably the easiest he was going to take. Once my blood was completely out of him the real pain would begin.

Chapter Eleven

Hendrix

I walked around with no place in mind. I didn't know where I was going so, I couldn't really have a place to go. Lalbert was no Melbourne. It was more like a big town rather than a city. It had everything that someone could need, but as far as places to get lost in, there wasn't a place. Unless you counted the forested areas that seemed to surround the town. I could get lost in there.

One thing I discovered is the supernatural population was by far greater than what I'd been expecting. It seemed just about every second person was supernatural. I passed a huge building that looked like a school. A guy stood out the front and tipped his head to me. I gave him a quick wave and kept moving. Beside the school was the police precinct. I kept my head down and moved past there quickly. I hadn't had much luck with cops. Maybe Lalbert's cops were a little different, but in Melbourne, most of them were pricks who looked down their noses at supernatural junkies.

Beyond that, there was a plethora of stores, clothing stores, tattoo salons, cafes, and a supermarket. The town was bustling even for being as small as it was. I'd slowly wandered past every store and looked in the window. Brenton's offer was still firmly in my mind. If I got clean, I could perhaps get a job, I could do something with my life. I might even one day set down roots. The sheer thought of that filled me with disbelief.

If the people who got their hands on me as a kid could see me thinking like that, they'd beat the shit out of me. But the truth is that they weren't here anymore. I hadn't been around them in an exceptionally long time. For the first time in my entire life, I was free. I was in a place where no one knew me. No one knew my past. I could become anybody that I wanted to be.

I kept walking through the streets until my stomach started to growl again, reminding me that I had only eaten what Brenton made me in the last few days. I walked back along the main street before coming across a small café called Tabby's. It looked like it would be an affordable place to eat. I still had twenty dollars in my pocket.

"Hi there, are you gonna come in?" a woman with a bright smile asked.

I bit in my bottom lip and nodded my head. "I've got, twenty dollars, what can I get for that?" I asked her quietly as a blush covered my cheeks.

The woman smiled and waved me over to a booth seat. "You pick whatever you like on there, it's on me today. I'm Tabby. What's your name?"

"Oh, I can pay, I just need to know what is cheap, I um, I can't read very well," I explained with embarrassment.

"What's your name?" she asked again.

I ducked my head. "Hendrix."

"It's lovely to meet you, Hendrix, now, I can highly recommend our chicken burger and fries. You can do a deal with a burger, chips, and a can of coke for seven dollars."

My eyes widened. "Oh, oh wow, that's cheap, yeah alright, can I please have that?"

Tabby smiled and nodded her head. "Sure thing. I'll bring your drink over and the food won't be too far away."

I smiled and glanced around the café. Everyone I'd met seemed so friendly. *Was it possible that Lalbert was filled with such friendly people?* That couldn't be possible. Surely. It didn't take long before Tabby came back with my burger and fries. My eyes bulged out of my head when I saw the size of it.

"If you can't eat it all, I'll pack the rest up for you to take with you," Tabby said as she placed the food in front of me. "Lots of people tell me my meals are too big. But I'm mated to a big old bear shifter."

I smiled up at her. "Thank you. I really appreciate that."

"Do you mind if I sit for a while?" she asked.

"Yeah, sure," I said feeling my cheeks blush again. Tabby slid into the booth opposite me as I bit into one of the fries. The greasy and salty taste had me humming with appreciation.

"Are you new here?" she asked.

I swallowed the bite I'd just taken of the burger and nodded my head. "Yeah. I arrived yesterday. I um, well I don't really know where I'm going."

Tabby smiled and nodded her head. "I was once just like you, you know."

I frowned and cocked my head to the side. "How so?"

"Well, I came to Lalbert when I was twenty. I was running from Melbourne," she said with a chuckle and shook her head. "I was a hooker. So drug addicted I could barely put one foot in front of the other. I don't even know how I managed to get on the bus let alone arrive here. Anyway, I got here and just wandered the streets. I didn't have any money in my pocket. I was starving, I was withdrawing like a bitch. I tried selling my body to people and got picked up by the AJE authority. Spent the night locked up. Kade Sinclair the head of the AJE authority, sat me down and told me that he would give me a choice. I could either stay in Lalbert and with his help get clean, or I could be put on the first bus out of the town. I was fuming. I was young with a huge chip on my shoulder. In the end, I realized that this was an opportunity of a lifetime. So, I took Kade up on his offer. He took me home to his mate; Merza and I went through the motions of getting clean."

"So, how did you manage to go from there to owning a café?" I asked in shock as I heard Tabby's story. Looking at her I would have never thought that was the life she'd come from.

Tabby smiled. "I'd been clean for a few months, and I said to Merza that I wanted a job. She brought me into town and introduced me to some of the store owners. Anyway, I met Eric, he owns a café down the road. He gave me a job and I worked hard, saving everything I earned. Then I met my mate, Michael. And well things just went up from there."

"That's amazing," I said as I took the last bite of my burger. I looked down with wide eyes as I realized I'd literally inhaled everything on the plate.

Tabby chuckled. "You were hungry. Want some dessert? On me."

I shook my head and leaned back in my seat rubbing my hands over my belly. "I couldn't fit anything else in. But thank you."

Tabby smiled. "Have you got somewhere to stay tonight?"

I nodded my head. "Yeah. I um, I met a guy named Brenton last night. He made me an offer the same as Kade made you."

Tabby's smile grew. "I know Brenton. He is a good man. A tattoo artist. He did these for me," she said as she pulled the sleeve of her shirt up so I could see the intricate artwork that dotted over her arm. "I had some scars I wanted covering and he did a beautiful job."

"They sure are beautiful," I said with a nod of my head.

"Brenton will help you if you let him."

I nodded my head again. I just had to let him.

Chapter Twelve

B renton
I could see that Hendrix was starting to come down from the blood that I'd given him. He was sitting on my couch but starting to scratch at his skin.

"What made you decide to come back?" I asked.

Hendrix looked up at me and sighed. "I met a lady named Tabby."

I smiled. I knew Tabby and I knew her story. It resembled Hendrix's story what I knew of his anyway.

"She is a great person."

"She said the same thing about you," Hendrix said with a smile.

I chuckled. "She only likes me for my artwork."

"I saw what you did for her, it was awesome."

I smiled again. "It's my life. I was extremely fortunate to be taken in by a wonderful man many years ago and taught everything."

"Like you are offering me?"

I shrugged my shoulders. "Similar. I wasn't drug addicted. But I was homeless, trying to sell my art. Barney, the man who took me in found me and brought me back to his house. He mentored me in art until the day he died. I decided from that time that I wanted to reach out and help others who had a rough start in life. I've lived all over the world before settling in Lalbert."

"How many people like me have you met?" Hendrix asked.

I shrugged. "I can't say for sure. There have been a lot. Some that just needed a shower and something to eat. Others like you needed help coming off the drugs and then some just needed some help to get a place to live in."

Hendrix nodded his head. "And in Lalbert?"

I smiled. "Well, there have been a few over the years. Tabby was already clean by the time I met her. But we get a fair number of transients coming through that live down on the river for a time. I take them food and supplies if they need them. There are only two living down there now. I make sure they are safe and that they have protection. But I make the same offer to any that are down there that are drug addicted. Some choose to take me up on the offer, others don't want to get off the drugs."

"How many have rolled you for what you have?"

I chuckled. "A few. But it's just stuff. Yeah, it's annoying and sometimes it hurts because I trusted them, but a TV is easy to replace."

Hendrix nodded and scratched at his chin. "So, what do you expect me to do?"

"Be committed. It's not going to be easy. You are going to go through withdrawals. You are going to hurt, but once you are through it, I will help you get housing if you want it, I can help you get a job. I can protect you."

Hendrix sat staring at me silently. I wondered what was going through his mind. Slowly he nodded his head. "I'm not sure you can promise me protection."

"What are you running from?" I asked.

Hendrix sighed and shook his head. "I saw something I shouldn't have seen."

I nodded my head and sighed. "And they are after you?"

Hendrix shrugged his shoulders. "I don't know for sure. They chased me but I managed to hide and then got on the bus and just came here. I don't know if they will keep looking for me or just forget about me."

"Will you tell me who?"

Hendrix shook his head. "Na. Maybe one day. But not today."

I nodded. "That's fair. I will organize to take some time off work to get you through the next couple of weeks. That's when it's going to be the hardest to come off the drugs. After that, we can see what you need."

"Alright. What if I can't do it? What if I need the drugs?"

"You will need the drugs. That is what addiction is."

Hendrix scoffed and shook his head. "So, what is the point?"

"Look you are always going to have this addiction," I said with air quotes. "It's never going to leave you and it will always be an easy route to fall back onto. But it will take strength on your part to fight those demons. I'm prepared to walk beside you, but I can't do it for you."

Hendrix sighed and nodded his head. He rubbed his hands up over his face and sunk back into the couch. "I don't know if I'm strong enough."

"If you want it badly enough, you will be strong. You will get through it. Lean on me. Tell me when it's too much, let me help you with the burden."

Hendrix sighed again and chewed on his bottom lip before nodding his head. "Alright. I'll try."

I smiled. "That's all I ask."

Chapter Thirteen

Hendrix

I woke up in the middle of the night, my skin felt like it was crawling with bugs. I was itchy everywhere. I was in full withdrawal and desperately wanted something to take the edge off. I moved my restless legs, my eyes felt swollen, my tongue felt like it was too big for my mouth, and I ached everywhere.

I stood from the bed and went into the hallway, glancing at the bathroom I wondered if Brenton had something in there that might just take the edge off. I went into the bathroom and flipped the light on. Looking at myself in the mirror I could see the pain I was in. My skin was pale, and my eyes were red and watering. I groaned as pain swept over my body. Nausea filled my stomach and I gagged. Leaning over the basin I dry retched. I opened the cabinet above the basin but there was nothing other than toiletries inside.

The bathroom door opened, and I looked up in the mirror to see Brenton standing in the doorway.

"It hurts," I groaned. "Please, can I have something?"

Brenton shook his head and stepped into the bathroom. He reached over the bath and flipped the taps on, feeling the water with his hand. He picked up a bottle of something and poured it into the bath. The scent of the forest filled the air. I stood watching him as my skin itched and my stomach ached.

"Get undressed," he directed. I didn't have the energy to fight his alpha that rippled through the room. In any other circumstance, I would have told him to go fuck himself, but I just wanted everything to stop hurting.

I slipped my shirt off over my head and pulled my boxers down. I stood watching Brenton, expecting him to touch me. He wouldn't be the first. Instead, he reached his hand out and took my hand in his. He led me over to the bath and guided me into the tub. The warmth in the water seemed to chase the bugs away instantly and I sighed.

"Sit down, the oils are a special blend, witch and warlock magic, it will help with the withdrawals," Brenton instructed.

I sunk down into the warm water and closed my eyes. Suddenly the pain eased. The bugs were no longer climbing over my skin, and I felt like I was floating on a cloud of peace.

"What is this?" I asked, blinking my eyes open.

"Merza Sinclair, she is the mate of the AJE authority top man, Kade. She is an immensely powerful witch, when she found out that I was helping those that were drug-addicted, she and one of the Devil's Advocates members, Oakland, who is a warlock created this bath oil, it helps to take away the symptoms of withdrawal without giving you the drugs. It will only last for a few hours once you get out of the bath, but if you need another one, take as many baths as you need until you are through it."

I closed my eyes again and sighed. "Thank you," I whispered. "What do you want from me in return."

"Your health. I want you to get healthy, I want to see you succeed, that is all I want in return."

I blinked my eyes open and shook my head. That couldn't be right, no one took nothing for something. Life didn't work that way.

Brenton glanced down at me and smiled. "You will soon see. You don't owe me, that's not how this works."

I shook my head. "That's how it works for everyone."

Brenton smiled but didn't say anything, before standing. "I'll leave you to your bath and come back and check you in a little while to make sure you don't fall asleep. I've pulled you out of the water once already, I'd rather not do that again."

I gave Brenton an uncertain smile and nodded my head as the vampire left the room, closing the door quietly behind him. I didn't get it. He wasn't like anyone I'd ever met before. He hadn't tried to touch me. I was laying there completely naked in front of him, and he didn't even glance at my cock. All supernaturals by nature were at least bisexual, but I guessed he could have been the exception. Not that my cock could have even got hard if I tried. I hadn't had a hard-on in an exceptionally long time. The drugs took that away.

I sighed and sunk deeper into the bath. I didn't know how long this setup with Brenton was going to last and I would be stupid if I didn't have an escape plan for when it all went tits up. But for right now, I needed to just soak in the bath and enjoy the fact that I wasn't hurting. It wasn't going to last forever.

Chapter Fourteen

B renton

It had been two weeks. There were a few days when I wondered if Hendrix was going to make it through, but he surprised me. Even though he was craving like crazy he stuck to it. He was down from around ten baths a day to just needing one or two. I was so proud of him. I was about to have to go back to work and I would be lying if I said I wasn't a little bit nervous about leaving him on his own.

He hadn't completely opened to me about his story, other than that he'd been on the streets since he was five years old. Fucking five years old. He was a fucking kid. It made me sick knowing that a kid that young had to try and navigate the world on their own. Unfortunately, though, his story was all too fucking common. World over. It made me sick to my stomach.

I still didn't know who he was running from. I'd assumed that it was a drug dealer, usually, that is how addicts found themselves on the run. They owed money or did something stupid. Though he told me that he'd seen something he shouldn't have, which made me curious. I'd thought about contacting Kade Sinclair to see if he knew but decided not to meddle. If Hendrix wanted me to know, he would tell me.

I got up every morning and prepared breakfast for us both, he usually tried to nap mid-morning, and then I would make him lunch. He was starting to look better. His face was getting some color in it, and he appeared to have put on a bit of weight. His jeans that desperately needed replacing were starting to fit him slightly more snuggly. I hadn't mentioned to him about buying him more clothes, I could tell from the last two weeks that despite his situation he was a proud man. He didn't like handouts. He was fiercely independent. I guessed that came from being on the streets since he was five.

"Morning," Hendrix mumbled as he stumbled into the kitchen, going straight for the coffee pot. It was his new addiction. But I figured it was much healthier than heroin.

"Morning. Did you sleep well?" I asked. I had been keeping an ear out for him over the last two weeks, last night was the first night I didn't hear the bath running in the middle of the night.

Hendrix smiled and nodded his head. "I slept all night, and I don't hurt this morning."

"That's great. It sounds like you are making it through to the other side."

Hendrix smiled but I could see that he was unsure. I didn't say anything, giving him the space to speak his mind.

"Um, so what happens when I don't need the drugs anymore?" he asked as he turned his back to pour his coffee.

I smiled; I had wondered when this conversation was going to come up. With Adam, it was instant. He felt like he needed to pay me for my help. It was the life of someone growing up a hard life, they learned exceedingly early on that you get nothing for nothing. But it was a worldview I wanted to change.

"Well, that depends on what you want and need. The way I see it you have a few options," I replied.

Hendrix turned to look at me with a small frown on his face as if he hadn't expected that answer. He moved over to the table where I sat, and pulled the chair out, sitting down opposite me.

"What are my options?" he asked.

"Option one is that you can leave here and move on and try to stay clean. Option two is that you can get a job in Lalbert, and I can help you to get a place of your own. Option three is that you can stay here and get a job and save until you can afford a house of your own."

Hendrix's frown deepened and he shook his head. "So, you're not going to chuck me out?"

"Of course not. That would be a waste of my time if I just threw you out there to the wolves. If I did that, I could guarantee that you'd end up back on drugs within the week."

Hendrix sighed and nodded his head. "Yeah, you're probably right. I don't have any job experience though. I've never worked, I can't even read beyond a third-grade level."

I nodded and gave him a smile. "What about school? How would you feel about going back and getting an education?"

Hendrix snorted. "I think I'd stand out if I went to the closest primary school and started in the third grade."

I chuckled and shook my head. "I wasn't thinking of a mainstream school. The Devil's Advocates have a lot of supernaturals who were saved from breeding facilities. Many of them don't know how to read. They don't know how to even do life. I was thinking more if you were interested in learning how to read better and to learn a trade, then maybe you could go out there. You don't have to take me up on that, the decision is always yours."

Hendrix hummed and he nodded his head. "Would they accept me though? I mean I don't ride a motorbike. I don't belong to the MC."

"One beautiful thing about the Devil's Advocates is that they accept everyone. If you are a good person and are willing to pitch in, they will take you in."

Hendrix bit into his lip and nodded. He ran his finger around the rim of his mug and stared down into the coffee.

"Maybe. Will you introduce me to the people that I need to ask if I can join with?"

I smiled. "Of course. Anghus is the president. He is mated to one of the AJE authority detectives, Bacchus, and an omega Joachim, who was in a breeding facility that the AJE authority broke down."

Hendrix frowned again. "They didn't take advantage of him?"

I shook my head. "I don't know all of their story, my boss Burgess, is Bacchus's brother, but they were fated mates."

Hendrix snorted and shook his head. "I don't believe in fate."

I smirked. "Me neither, but sometimes I kinda wonder. Don't you wonder why you got on that bus that was driven by one of my mates? Why do you just happen to start to drown in the river just down from me? Why did a doctor just happen to be on the bank that night."

Hendrix looked at me and frowned. "Yeah, that makes sense. I'm not sure I'm meant to have someone though."

I shrugged my shoulders. "I can't answer that. Vampires don't have fated mates. That is something for shifters. And I don't know enough about broonies to know about you."

Hendrix shrugged his shoulders. "That makes two of us. All I know about being a broonie is that I can shrink and that always came in handy. Beyond that, I know nothing."

"Well, that is something that the Devils can help you with. They are very much about learning the heritage of a supernatural and teaching each supernatural to learn about themselves."

"So, they might be able to help me find out what happened to my parents?"

I was shocked by his question; it was the first time that Hendrix had mentioned his parents. I nodded my head. "Yep. There is a dragon shifter who works with the AJE authority, her name is Arcadia. She works alongside the Devil's as well; she is the record keeper for all the supernaturals."

Hendrix shook his head. "I don't want anything to do with a dragon."

I noticed that his hands had started to tremble. I frowned but nodded my head. "You don't have to have anything to do with her. I'm not here to push you to do anything you aren't ready for."

"Except to give up drugs," Hendrix replied with a wry smile.

"Apart from that," I chuckled. "And you have done incredibly."

"Thanks. I owe you a lot."

I shook my head. "As I said, the only thing I ask in payment is that you go on to do well, stay off the drugs and make something of your life."

Hendrix sighed and nodded his head before staring back down at his coffee. "I'll try. I'll think about the Devil's. I feel a bit overwhelmed."

"Take your time. You're not being hurried yet."

Hendrix smiled but didn't look up at me.

Chapter Fifteen

H endrix

Brenton had been right; quitting hadn't been easy. I think it was the hardest thing I'd ever faced. It took two weeks before I even started to feel like I'd come through the worst of it. The bath oil was a life send; I didn't know how I would have coped if I didn't have that. I would have crumbled and gone to find some dealers, is what I would've done.

Now I was facing a decision. I didn't know what to do. Brenton had presented me with several options. I was still waiting for the other shoe to drop. I was waiting for that moment that he would decide I needed to pay up. I felt myself sitting on the edge the entire time waiting. But night after night, he never came to claim payment. Brenton would say good night to me every night and then I wouldn't see him once he went to his room. I couldn't work it out. He wasn't like anyone I'd ever met before.

The fear that Cillian was coming after me was starting to ease. I hadn't really left the house, so I didn't hear whispers of him coming into town. I felt safe in the house from the outside forces. But I was still so used to the street that I was in a constant state of waiting. Waiting for that moment when someone tried to take something from me.

Brenton had gone to work, leaving me home with nothing but my thoughts. The cravings had eased. They still were there, but so quiet that I could easily ignore them. I guessed that those cravings were going to always be there, and I didn't believe for a minute that I would ever be able to walk away and never be tempted to go back. But it was something I knew I was going to have to remain strong with.

I sat on the couch in the living room of Brenton's house and stared out the window. My head was filled with the options that Brenton had given me that morning. The thought of being welcomed as part of the Devil's Advocates was appealing. To learn to read and write better than

I could. To have the opportunity to get a career one day. It was like a dream that had always been too out of reach, and I wondered if it was possible.

The other option I had was to try and get a job. I had a feeling if I asked Tabby, I might be able to get work there. But I wasn't confident that I would be much good at any job. My whole life had been spent just trying to survive. I huffed out a breath and closed my eyes. I didn't know what the answer was.

Slapping my knees, I stood and looked for my shoes that were next to the front door. The thought of having a job and being able to buy clothes and have somewhere to keep them was tempting. Slipping my shoes on, I opened the front door. I locked it behind me. I didn't have a way to get back in, but I didn't mind sitting on the front step until Brenton got home. I needed fresh air. I needed to get my head right.

I walked down the driveway. Last time I'd gone right, taking me into the city. I chose this time to go left instead and head into the forest. Maybe there would be a trail that I could walk along. It was strange going for a walk while I was sober. Suddenly the sounds, colors, scents, and feel of the outside world were crisper. It wasn't hidden behind a drug haze. I liked it.

A small smile crept across my lips as I walked towards the tree line I could see in the distance. Once I reached the end of the road, I saw a sign that said it led to Lalbert River. I wondered if this was the river I'd nearly died in when Brenton found me.

I still had no memory of that night. I think it was a mix of fear, the drugs, and the head injury that stripped me of the memory. I started down the dirt path towards the river. The birds sang to one another in the trees and a cool breeze whipped around me, causing goosebumps to prickle on my arms.

"Hendrix?" a man said as he stepped out of the tree line.

I gasped and halted. My heart started to ricochet in my chest and my need to run was kicking in.

The man held his hands up. "Not a threat. My name is Ryan. I'm friends with Brenton. That's how I know your name."

I let out a slow breath and nodded my head. I wasn't sure whether to trust his word or not. I glanced around me to see if he was alone. Ryan came towards me with a wary smile.

"You're clean?"

I nodded my head. "Yeah."

Ryan's smile grew. "Good. You met the protector, and you took him up on his offer. I'm glad for you. I'll see you around."

With that Ryan turned and walked away into the trees. I stood frowning at the back of Ryan as he disappeared into the trees. I shook my head unsure what the hell just happened. I glanced around me again and didn't see anyone. I let out a slow breath and started towards the river again. In the distance, I could see two tents. I remembered Brenton saying that there were homeless that lived down at the river. I followed the path until I reached the river.

I sat down on the bench seat that stood at the edge of the river. Staring out at the water, I watched as dragonfly's danced on the surface. Closing my eyes, I soaked in the sun that warmed my face. I felt good. For the first time in an exceptionally long time, I felt good. I wasn't sure how long it was going to last, but I would take it for as long as that good feeling stuck around.

Chapter Sixteen

B renton

I'd be lying if I didn't say I was curious to see what decision Hendrix would make. Personally, I kind of hoped he chose to stay. I didn't know what it was about him, but I liked him. I wasn't about to try and launch myself at him. I mean he was hot, but that was a lot of supernaturals. There was something about him that drew me to him. I couldn't explain what it was. If I was a shifter, I might have thought it was fate. But I wasn't a shifter, and I didn't believe that we were fated. For one, Hendrix was an alpha. Not that it mattered it seemed. It worked for Anghus and Bacchus.

My head was full of thoughts while I went through the motions of tattooing. I was glad that my clients only wanted small easy tattoos because I didn't think I could focus long enough to do an excellent job.

"What's going on with you?" Chase, one of the other tattooists, asked as I sighed again while I cleaned up my station after the third butterfly tattoo for the day.

"I don't know. Hendrix is through the worst of the withdrawals. I gave him his options. But I don't know what it is, I'm almost feeling afraid that he will choose to leave," I said with a small shrug of my shoulders.

"Does he know that you feel that way?" Chase asked.

I shook my head. "Na. He is constantly waiting for me to take from him as payment. I didn't want him to think that's what my feelings were."

Chase winced and nodded his head. "Yeah, that makes things a little tricky. Has he given you a hint about how he is feeling?"

I shook my head. "I know he doesn't want to go back to Melbourne. He is running from someone there, I don't know who, all he told me was that he saw something he wasn't meant to see. But I'm not sure if he will want to stay in Lalbert. Compared to Melbourne there isn't a lot here."

Chase nodded and leaned back against my bench and crossed his arms over his chest. He was a fellow vampire who was of a similar age. He didn't talk a whole lot about the life he'd lived. I know that he grew up in a rough neighborhood in Melbourne. He was bullied a lot by the humans that lived in the area. But unlike me, he grew up with wonderful parents who loved him. He was a great sounding board. Out of everyone that I worked with Chase, and I were the closest.

"It's a tricky situation that you find yourself in. What are the options that you gave him?"

"I told him the standard talk of he could leave, he could stay and get a job and I'd help him find a place in Lalbert, or he could stay with me until he could afford to get his own place. But when he told me that he'd only been able to read at a third-grade level, I suggested that he go out to the Devil's compound and do some education classes with the omegas out there."

Chase rubbed at his chin and nodded his head. "Yeah, that's a clever idea. What did he say?"

"He just told me that he needed to think about it."

Chase chuckled. "So, he really isn't giving anything away. Well, I'm hoping that he chooses to go to the Devil's. They are good people. He will find a lot that shares commonality with him."

I nodded my head. I knew that several members had come from drug addiction. Some were prostitutes, dealers and had a lot of trouble in their past. I knew that if he gave them a chance Hendrix would be able to find people that completely understood his situation. I also knew that he would be protected out there. And selfishly it also meant that I would get the chance to see him still.

The door to the shop tinkled and Anghus walked in. I chuckled and shook my head. "Well speak of the devil himself," I laughed.

Anghus stopped and cocked his head to the side. "I wondered why my ears were burning."

I laughed and patted the seat. Anghus stepped into my booth and sat down. "What can I do for you?"

"I was hoping that you might have some time for some work, if not I can book in with you," he replied.

I glanced up at the clock, I had two hours until my next client was due, which would give me a chance to give Anghus a smallish tattoo. I could at least get some outline work done for whatever he wanted. It would also give me a chance to pick his brain about Hendrix.

"What are you looking for?" I asked.

"The kid's names," he said pointing at his chest.

"Easy, I can do that. Let's get started," I said as I turned to draw up the names of his kids. Iver and McKenna.

Chapter Seventeen

Hendrix

I sat on the park bench for hours just listening to the birds and soaking in the sunshine. It felt so good to sit there and not crave, not be stoned, to be completely sober, and just enjoy the world around me. I took in every sound, scent, and color that carried on the wind. By the time my stomach was growling and ready to head back I noticed that the sky was starting to dance with a sea of pink and purple. It was colors that in the city of Melbourne you didn't see. Hidden by the skyscrapers and smog.

I sighed a deep breath and stood from my seat before turning to head back towards Brenton's house. I wasn't any closer to a decision. Or maybe I was and just didn't realize it. I didn't want to leave Brenton. The very thought of it worried me. At first, I thought it was that I used Brenton as a crutch. He was the one that helped me get clean so I saw that I couldn't do life without him. But the more I thought about it, the more I realized that it wasn't like that.

I knew I could do life without Brenton. I knew that I would never return to Melbourne, but I could move anywhere. I could live anywhere, if I stayed clean, I could do anything I wanted. But I didn't want to leave Brenton. There was something about the vampire. It was like he had so much left to teach me, and I had so much more to learn from him.

My mind moved over each option Brenton had given me as I walked back towards his home. I couldn't move away; I could easily scratch that one off the option list. I wasn't ready to leave Lalbert yet. Sure, I'd only been here a brief time and didn't know anything about the town, but it already held a sentimental part of my heart. It was the first place I ever got clean. That meant something. So, moving away wasn't an option.

The second option was to move out of Brenton's home and get a job. That was something I could do. Brenton offered to help me to get a house and a job. I knew that if I spoke to Tabby then she would likely hire me. Not to mention that there were plenty of other places where I could work. How well I could do was another story. But that option was there. The other one was that I stay with Brenton and get a job but stay with him until I can afford to move out on my own.

That was an appealing option too. But the last option was the one that held so much intrigue for me. Go to the Devil's Advocates and learn. Attend school with other omegas and alphas that had been through similar things as me. Make friends. People I could trust. In truth, I didn't know if that was what would happen at all. For all I knew, the Devil's Advocates would completely reject me, but something in my gut told me that it wouldn't be like that. I'd learned to trust my gut after all these years on the streets.

I walked up the front path of Brenton's house and noticed that his car wasn't in the driveway, so I sat down on the front step to wait for him. Chewing on my bottom lip I continued to think over everything again. The more I thought about things the more I wanted to trust Brenton. I wanted to settle. That was weird to me. I'd never wanted to settle in a place before. Mainly because I never saw a point. The only reason I stayed in Melbourne for as long as I did was that Rick lived there and supplied me with drugs.

Now I didn't have that to hold me to a place. Maybe Cillian did me a favor. Maybe Lalbert could be my new home. I didn't know. I hummed in my throat and rested my chin on my knees as I stared out over the front garden.

I was still staring out at the front garden when a black car pulled into the driveway. It wasn't Brenton's car and when I lifted my head my breath caught in my throat. I stood and was about to run when I spotted the silver flash that caught the light. A gun barrel pointed straight at me. I may have been able to outrun Cillian, but I couldn't outrun a bullet.

"Hello Hendrix," Cillian purred as he stepped out of the car and walked towards me.

"Please, I'm trying to make a new life here. I'm clean, I haven't said anything to anyone," I pleaded.

Cillian stopped and nodded his head. I almost thought he was considering what I was saying, but the look in his eye told me that my pleas was ignored. He didn't care. As far as the dragon shifter was concerned, I was a problem. And as I saw with Rick, problems had to be eradicated.

My heart broke in my chest. I sent out a prayer to the universe that Brenton wouldn't come home. The last thing I needed was for him to get caught up in something that was my fault.

"I'm glad you haven't said anything Hendrix, but how long will that last? How long before you decide to blabber to someone, to the vampire you've housed up with? Hmm?" Cillian sneered.

I shook my head. "I haven't said anything to him. He has no idea. Please Cillian, go back to Melbourne, I'll stay here, and you won't have to ever see me again."

Cillian shook his head. "That's just not how this works Hendrix."

Cillian stepped forward with a speed I didn't anticipate. I stood no chance. I didn't even have time to shift before his big meaty hands clasped hold of my upper arms and I suddenly felt a prick of a needle sink itself into my neck.

My eyes rolled in my head as I got the distinct rush of heroin that I'd worked so hard to overcome. I felt myself sink into that all too familiar feeling. Except for this time, it was too much. He'd given me too much. I was about to overdose. My heart pounded and I felt nausea wash over me. My eyes rolled to the back of my head, and I cried out as vomit spewed from my mouth and drenched the front of my shirt.

Darkness crept to the edges of my vision, and I knew that unless I got some Narcan soon, I was going to die. This was it. All that work, all that hope. Gone in an instant. Darkness took over, just as I heard a deafening bang and felt my body crumple. My head slammed against the hard concrete and the darkness took control. That was it. I was dead.

Chapter Eighteen

B renton
I pulled into a shitshow happening at my house after work. I got out of the car with wide eyes and complete confusion. There were AJE authority members all over my front yard. Doc was screaming at Ryan, who was handcuffed and being held by Memphis a shifter detective. Three men lay bleeding on the front lawn near a black car.

"Where is Hendrix?" I said looking around for the broonie.

"Adam has him, he is alright now, I was able to bring him back to life," Doc said.

"What the hell?" I roared as my heart leaped into my throat. "Where? Where is he?"

"He is with the medics," Doc answered pointing at the ambulance. I turned and jogged towards the ambulance and saw that Hendrix was laid on the bed, tears soaked his cheeks that were so pale.

"Brenton," Adam said with a sad shake of his head.

'What the hell happened?" I asked with shock in my voice.

"Hendrix is alright with the medics, come with me so we can talk without upsetting him further," Adam said pulling on my arm. I didn't want to leave the ambulance; I was in a complete state of confusion. *What was going on?*

Adam took me to the side of the ambulance; I could still hear the medics talking quietly to Hendrix and him answering.

"Adam, what is going on?" I asked.

"I was coming back from work and caught what happened. Hendrix was talking to the guy, one of the dead ones over there," he said motioning with his chin. "The big guy grabbed Hendrix and injected him with something. Hendrix tried to get away, but the big guy was too strong. Whatever he injected Hendrix with sent him into an overdose. I ran and got Doc. He had Narcan still from when I was using and was able to bring it to give Hendrix, which stopped the overdose."

I frowned and shook my head. "Who are those guys and how did they end up dead?"

"The big guy is Cillian Purcell, he is a big-time dealer in Melbourne, I'd say that's who your boy was running from. He is a dragon shifter and a real piece of shit; I knew of him when I was in Melbourne but tried to stay clear from him. If you cross him, you can consider yourself dead and if he has you in your sights he doesn't stop until he gets you."

"So, how is he dead?" I asked with a shake of my head.

"Ryan. I don't know where he materialized from, but he came in and killed Cillian and his men within a blink of an eye, which happened before I even ran for Doc."

I scrubbed my hands up over my face. "How did Cillian know where Hendrix was. He hasn't left the house in two weeks."

"Also, Ryan."

"What the fuck?"

"Ryan works for Cillian or worked for Cillian. I don't know the whole story; I just know that Ryan owed Cillian for something. Anyway, Ryan saw that Hendrix was still around when Hendrix went for a walk today down to the river and let Cillian know."

Fury like I'd never felt before welled up inside me. I turned and felt my fangs elongate. I glared at Ryan who looked over at me. He dropped his head and nodded. Within seconds I was standing beside Ryan and had his throat in my hand. I wanted to tear his throat from his neck.

"I'm sorry Brenton. Kill me, I deserve it," he said.

"Brenton, stop," I heard someone growl. The alpha tone in that statement had me dropping Ryan. I spun on the person that had dared to use their alpha on me to face Kade Sinclair. The only other man that could be strong enough to stop me.

"He will be punished, do not get yourself in trouble by killing him," Kade said.

"He nearly had Hendrix killed," I growled in return.

Kade nodded his head. "I know. And I know that you're angry for your mate but killing him isn't going to solve this. You need to be here for your mate."

I stood with the wind knocked out of my sails. My mate. It couldn't be possible. But I'd never reacted so strongly towards someone before. I sighed out a breath and blinked my eyes closed. I nodded my head and turned back to Ryan who was watching me with tears in his eyes.

"You are never to come back here, if you don't get sent down for this, you are to leave and never return, do you understand?" I growled.

Ryan nodded his head. "I will."

I turned away and went back to the ambulance that was still sitting at the edge of the curb. Ignoring everyone I climbed into the back of the ambulance and reached out my hand to take Hendrix's in mine.

"I didn't take the drugs on purpose Brenton," Hendrix said with tears in his eyes.

"I know, love, I know. Adam explained it all to me," I replied as I brought his knuckles to my lips and kissed them.

Hendrix sighed. "You're not mad at me?"

I shook my head and gave him a smile. "Not in the least. I'm scared, I'm worried but I'm not mad."

Hendrix nodded. "Can I stay with you?"

"For as long as you want," I replied.

Hendrix breathed out a deep sigh and squeezed my hand. I hoped that he would stay forever.

Chapter Nineteen

Hendrix

Once the medics released me as being fine, I'd gone inside with Brenton and curled up in bed and slept for the rest of the night. I didn't know what to think. I had nearly died at the hand of Cillian and then a drug dealer killed him. I just didn't know what to make of it all. Had it not been for Adam, and Doc I would have died. I wanted to thank them, but I was so tired.

The following morning, I woke up feeling sore, but at least I wasn't craving the drugs. My hands were shaking, and I was feeling jumpy.

"Good morning," Brenton said as he came into the room. He was another thing to think about. He'd called me love. He hadn't let me go. I'd agreed to stay with him. I didn't know what was going on. I heard him refer to me as my mate before I walked into the house. It was all too much to think about.

"Morning," I mumbled as I poured myself a cup of coffee and topped it with milk and five sugars. I sat down at the table and watched as Brenton moved his way around the kitchen.

"I've taken today off. Adam and Doc were pretty shaken up after yesterday so I said I would go down there and spend some time with them. Would you like to come?"

I nodded my head. "Yes. I want to thank them for saving my life."

Brenton winced but covered it quickly with a smile. I could still see the fear that was in his eyes. It was the same fear I'd seen when he was holding my hand in the back of the ambulance. Words people could fake, but that look in his eye, he couldn't fake that. It made me wonder if he was as confused as I was. I chewed on my bottom lip and sighed.

"Brenton?" I started. Brenton turned to face me and cocked his head to the side. "Can I talk to you about something?"

"Of course. You can tell me anything," he replied.

I nodded my head and pushed the chair out beside me so that he could come and sit beside me at the table.

"I um, I'm feeling a little confused about things. I'm probably going to make a complete cunt of myself right now, but what is happening between us? I mean, are we mates?" My cheeks tinted pink with embarrassment.

To my surprise, Brenton didn't laugh like I had expected him to. "How much do you know about supernaturals?"

I shrugged my shoulders. "Not a lot. I didn't grow up learning."

Brenton smiled and nodded his head. "Neither did I. It wasn't until I met Barney that I learned what it was to be supernatural and even now I learn new stuff every day. But in the supernatural world, there are mates, typically vampires don't have the fated mates that shifters have. But we do find ourselves drawn more strongly to people who are meant to be for us. So, in a way, I guess it is a mate. However, people don't become mates just like that. For shifters, they share a mating bite. For vampires, we often will share blood. I'm not sure for broonies, I'm afraid that is sort of out of my knowledge base, but I can find out."

I sat back and thought about it. "You gave me your blood," I pointed out remembering when he'd first found me dying.

Brenton nodded his head. "I did. However, that is a little different from how a mating bond works. During a mating bond, you would bite me or cut me if you don't have fangs and take from my blood, and I would take from you. When I gave you my blood, you didn't return the exchange, it was a way to save your life."

I nodded and chewed on my lip. "How do you know if someone is meant to be your mate?"

"Well, I can't say for sure. I've never met someone that I've felt that way about, well before now."

"How do you feel now?" I asked.

Brenton sucked in a deep breath and licked over his bottom lip. "I have felt a pull to you from the time I brought you home. I wanted to save you. I thought that was only because you were in trouble. But then when you were getting better, I started to realize I didn't want you to leave. However, yesterday. When I realized you were in danger I nearly went out of my mind. I wanted to kill Ryan for bringing Cillian to our door. I would have killed Cillian if he'd still been alive."

I smiled and nodded my head. "I think I understand. I have felt that pull to you too. Like it makes me feel sick if I think about going away. I went for a walk yesterday and just sat at the river thinking about everything. The thought of moving away wasn't even on the agenda, but then when I thought of even moving out of the house, I felt sick, like it was the worst idea ever."

Brenton smiled and nodded. "That's how I feel at the thought of you leaving too."

"So, does that mean we are meant to be mates?"

Brenton shrugged his shoulders. "I think that we are placed in each other's lives for a reason, however, I think we still have a choice. If you didn't want to mate with me or even have a mate, then you can say no, and I would never try to force myself on you."

I frowned and twisted my lips to the side. "But that isn't fair on you."

Brenton smiled. "The last thing I would ever want to do is make you feel trapped, love."

I smiled and sighed. "I don't feel trapped around you. I never have. I've been afraid of the feeling that we were getting closer, and I've taken a long time to trust you. But I know inside my heart that you are a good person. I know deep down that you'd never hurt me."

Brenton shook his head. "I would sooner die than hurt you."

I nodded. "I know. Would you want to be my mate?"

"Oh love, I'd be honored."

I smiled again. "I'd like to try. But only if you wanted to."

Brenton leaned forward and gently pressed his lips on mine. His lips were soft and warm as they moved over mine in small kisses. I poked my tongue out and licked at Brenton's lower lip causing him to moan. He opened his mouth and tangled his tongue with mine. I moved my head to the side and deepened our kiss. My heartbeat was wild in my chest, but it wasn't with fear. It was exciting. For the first time since the time I was born, I felt hope. Hope for a future that might be possible.

Chapter Twenty

B renton

Our kiss quickly turned from a sweet kiss to hot and heavy in a matter of seconds. Hendrix climbed out of his seat and straddled my lap. My hands stroked up and down over his back as he rolled his hips. His cock was hard as he pressed into me. My own cock was straining against my jeans. My brain was struggling to keep up with this sudden change in events, but my body was screaming at me to give him everything.

I broke the kiss reluctantly and looked up at Hendrix. "Are you sure that you want this, love?"

Hendrix bit into his bottom lip and nodded his head. "I want to belong Brenton. I want to be yours. I want you to be mine."

I smiled. The words were like a sweet blessing caress to my ears. I took Hendrix's hands in mine and guided him off my lap. Standing I led him behind me towards my bedroom. If we were going to do this, we were going to go slow, I was going to make him feel love. It wasn't going to be a quick fuck at my kitchen table.

"Have you ever bottomed before?" I asked as we reached my bedroom. Hendrix scrunched his nose and nodded his head. I chuckled. "I take it you didn't think much of it."

Hendrix shook his head. "No. It hurt. A lot."

I nodded my head. "Then they didn't do particularly good. But I'm versatile, I like bottoming as much as I like to top."

Hendrix smiled and seemed to breathe easier. Slowly I reached for the hem of his shirt and lifted it from his chest. From the first time I'd seen him to now, he had put on some weight and was looking so much healthier than he had been. His breathing was coming in choppy pants as I reached for the button on his jeans and slowly lowered them over his hips.

"You can stop at any time. You are not trapped here, if you don't want to do something, then just say the word and we stop," I said looking into his eyes to make sure he understood that he held the power.

Hendrix smiled up at me and nodded his head. "Thank you," he whispered. "I don't want to stop."

I smiled and reached out for his boxers, lowering them to the ground. His cock was straining hard. He was cut and the mushroom head was red and weeping. I lowered to my knees and opened my mouth, sucking his shaft over my tongue to the back of my throat.

Hendrix moaned as he thrust his hands into my hair and held on as I moved my mouth up and down the hardened length. His moans were a delight to listen to. I stroked my hands up his thighs and to his balls that I gently caressed with the tips of my fingers.

"Oh god," Hendrix moaned. "Oh fuck, fuck, you're going to make me cum."

I smiled around his cock and continued to suck as his fingers tightened in my hair. Hendrix cried out again as jets of cum sprayed into my mouth. Spray after spray I swallowed him down, delighting in the salty flavor as it burst on my tongue.

"Jesus," Hendrix moaned as I let his cock go with a pop and looked up at him. "I don't think I've ever had my cock sucked like that before."

I chuckled and stood. "I aim to please, love."

"I like it when you call me love."

My smile grew and I leaned forward pressing my lips against his. Hendrix moaned and stepped closer to my body, wrapping his arms around my back as our tongues tangled together. He lifted my shirt, and I broke the kiss long enough to allow him to lift it up off my head before his fingers went for the button and zipper of my jeans. Soon I was naked, and Hendrix was looking over my body with hooded lids.

"Are you sure you want to bottom?" he asked as he looked up at me with indecision.

"I'm positive," I replied with a smile before going to my bedside drawer and pulling out a bottle of lube. It was true what I said, I liked to bottom. I was happy with either.

I handed the lube to Hendrix who uncapped the bottle and poured a good amount into his hand before stroking it up and down his cock which was hard again. I took the lube from him and poured some on my fingers before prepping my hole. I lay back on the bed and lifted my legs, delving my fingers in and out of my ass while Hendrix watched me. His lips popped open, and his breathing sped up. His pupils were blown, and I knew the sight was affecting him. I let out a little moan as my fingers pressed on my prostate.

"Fuck, that is so sexy," Hendrix whispered. I didn't know how much experience Hendrix had, but none of that mattered. He was mine. We were going to make this life together forever on.

"Come and fuck me, love," I instructed.

Hendrix nodded his head and stepped between my legs. Gently he rolled the head of his cock up and down over my hole. I groaned at the feel of him. I wanted him, more than I ever wanted anyone.

Slowly Hendrix pushed inside me. I groaned and my eyes rolled in my head as his cock pressed on my prostate. Hendrix moaned and rolled his hips.

"It feels so good," he moaned as he leaned over me and continued to fuck into me.

"So, good," I moaned in response.

"Mate with me Brenton, please?" Hendrix pleaded.

I smiled and nodded my head. Pushing the nail to lengthen on my finger I ran it along my chest. A line bloomed with blood. "Feed, love," I instructed.

Hendrix immediately lowered his mouth over the wound, and I cried out in pleasure as his tongue swiped through the blood. "God, yes, suck on the wound," I cried.

Hendrix's hips are pistoned into me as he sucked on the cut, drinking down my blood. My fangs elongated and I leaned forward. I allowed my teeth to sink into Hendrix's soft neck. My mate roared as I felt his cock swell and fill me with his cum. Before I knew what was happening, I watched as Hendrix's teeth elongated and he answered my bite. It was too much and not enough all at once. I roared, my alpha shook the room, and jets of cum sprayed between the two of us.

I'd never felt anything like it. My whole body trembled under the weight of our mating. Hendrix sunk down onto my chest. I stroked my hand up over his back as I listened to our breaths even out.

"Wow," Hendrix whispered before lifting his head making me laugh.

"Yeah, love, that was definitely wow."

Hendrix laughed and kissed me gently.

Hendrix

My life was so good. I'd never expected it to end up the way it did when I first got on that bus. Hell, I was just hoping to be able to escape Cillian. I found out that Ryan, who was a drug dealer who unfortunately worked for Cillian had let the drug lord know where I was. Cillian then came to find me. But it was Ryan who killed him. I'd been curious to know whether he told Cillian where I was so that he could kill him, but I didn't know.

I'd attended Ryan's trial and spoke asking the judge to give him a lenient sentence. I don't think that Brenton agreed with me, but he killed my biggest nightmare. I was safe because of Ryan. If Ryan hadn't killed him, I would have died from an overdose that day. I mean I guess if Ryan hadn't told Cillian where I was, I wouldn't have had a run-in with the dragon shifter anyway, but it had worked out in the end.

The judge gave Ryan a twenty-year sentence in a human prison. According to Brenton, human prisons were safer and nicer than supernatural prisons. So, I was glad about that. I'd started getting to know Adam and Doc. I found out that the pair of them really enjoyed living down at the river and didn't want a house. They were an interesting pair. I still didn't know if they were mated or not, but they were lovely guys.

I also was getting to know all the people at Shifter Ink. I really liked them. Burgess was friendly. In fact, everyone that I had met in Lalbert was lovely. I'd started doing lessons at the Devil's Advocates compound. And I was learning to drive. Jai, one of the Devil's was teaching me.

It was amazing how similar my story was to many of the others. All these years I'd thought I'd had a horrible life that no one would understand but in truth, there were so many that knew.

Trudy who was a siren and a Devil had been found drug addicted by one of the other Devil's Israel, the sergeant at arms. He helped her get clean. Then there was Amber, a fae who had been a prostitute in the supernatural prisons. And yet here they were testaments to what good friends, family, and a little help could do.

I still didn't necessarily believe in fate, but I started to think that I was meant to have come to Lalbert. I was meant to have met Brenton and the Devil's Advocates. I was meant to have this life. It had started off in hell but was quickly becoming heaven.

I'd been blessed. Whether that was by the creator of Mother fate. Either way, I would happily take it.

The End.

Don't miss out!

Visit the website below and you can sign up to receive emails whenever S L Davies publishes a new book. There's no charge and no obligation.

https://books2read.com/r/B-A-NZRR-OFFBC

BOOKS 2 READ

Connecting independent readers to independent writers.

Also by S L Davies

Breeding Facility
Memphis
Bacchus
Coltrane
Pax
Raiden
Nash

Devil's Advocates
Lynx
Israel
Jai
Jasper
Arley
Zion
Oakland

KINK
Gunner
Newlyn

Freya
Tanquil

Obsidian Mechanics
Donte

Onyx Rebels
Onyx Rebels Prologue
Hawke

Rigby Brothers
Asher
Burgess
Macklin
Drake
Obsidian

Schiavu
Schiavu

Shifter Ink
Brenton

Standalone

Sisters Revenge
Killer Love
Soldiers At War
Second Chances
Bunny
Caged

About the Author

S L Davies is an Australian Author living in Country, Victoria. She is inspired by the world around her.

Read more at https://www.amazon.com/~/e/B0832T8F7Z.